~~THE AWESOME DOODLE~~

~~THE WORLD'S GREATEST SUPERHERO~~

SUPER DWEEB
AND
THE PENCIL OF DESTINY

By Jess Bradley

ARCTURUS

ARCTURUS

This edition published in 2022 by Arcturus Publishing Limited, 26/27 Bickels Yard, 151–153 Bermondsey Street, London SE1 3HA

Copyright © Arcturus Holdings Limited

Words and pictures: Jess Bradley
Design: Stefan Holliland
Original concept: Joe Harris
Art direction: Rosie Bellwood

ISBN: 978-1-78950-293-0
CH007132NT
Supplier 13, Date 0422, PI 00001563

Printed in China

Hi, I'm ANDY. Nice to meet you, person reading this! I'll call you P.R.T. for short. (You're cool with that, right, P.R.T.?) I'm a pretty normal kid. A bit dweeby, maybe. I can't catch a **football** or dance but I can draw pretty much ANYTHING. Except for hands, which are really hard. This is the incredible TRUE STORY of how I became a

SUPERHERO.

(Yes, really!)

LOOK! IT'S ME!

DOODLING

Andy? Andy!

CONTENTS

"Andy! ANDY! ANNNDDDDYYY! Are you paying attention

in class or are you DRAWING AGAIN?"

Uh-oh. This sounded like a problem that not even ACE SILVERBACK, maverick space-gorilla cop, could solve. I had been completely lost in thought, happily doodling the latest cosmic adventure in my awesome SPACE APE^{TM} series.

But I wasn't being threatened by evil alien octopods in the ghastly gamma quadrant. No, the truth was much worse—I was in Mr. Squibb's <u>MATH CLASS</u>. And Mr. Squibb did NOT look happy.

"The last time I checked, we were not studying ART. We were studying algebra. And these ... monkeys and squid ... are definitely NOT ALGEBRA!"

$4 \times 2 =$
$X = Y+7 =$

"Um, it's an ape and an octopus actually," I mumbled. " Not a squibb—I mean, a squid." Several of the class sniggered.

"I don't CARE!" said Mr. Squibb, "Drawing pictures won't get you anywhere in life."

Mr. Squibb is <u>SUPER-BORING</u>. If I had to write reports for my teachers, this is what I would send home to his parents.

MR. SQUIBB'S REPORT CARD
Your son, Mr. Squibb, has no imagination. Like, literally, zero. His favorite book is the dishwasher manual. He can suck the fun and excitement out of absolutely anything—like some kind of super-powerful fun vacuum cleaner. (Except that sounds sort of cool, so forget that.) Grade: ZZZ (for snoring).

"Are you paying attention, ANDY?" Somehow, Mr. Squibb was still speaking. "As I was saying—that's why today we will be taking a field trip. A highly educational field trip. Everyone take a leaflet and pass it on."

I took one of the leaflets and read it.

"We also have a new student! This is MONA . Why don't you tell us a little bit about yourself?"

"We moved here from Battsburg so my dad could study AI at the university. This town smells funny. <u>NOT GOOD FUNNY.</u>"

SO COOL!

"Um, super! Well, why don't you go and take a seat with Andy? In fact, you can be his BUDDY on the school trip!"

Of course everyone laughed. A COOL person being buddies with ME?

Tie (I like ties! They're fancy!)

Thick glasses (I like them).

Full of super interesting facts.

Most likely to join every school club.

Good at drawing (but not hands).

Hi, I'm Andy! Do you like comics?

Hrmpf.

I'm working on one! It's really fun! I like drawing but I'm not too good with hands!

SPACE APE!

I hope to be a comic artist one day, so I can doodle all day! Have you ever read the **Gamma Guys** graphic novel? I'll lend it to you!

Rah!

Beep!

Woo!

ICY STARE!

Um, did you know that human DNA is super close to mushroom DNA?

That would make me a real FUN-GUY!

???

Woo. Tough crowd.

"Hey, New Girl! Have fun being paired with UBER-DORK! Ha ha ha!"

GOOD ONE!

YEAH! DORK!

HA HA! HEE!

Ugh, it's Mean Mike! Every class has that one kid destined to be a super villain and Mike is in MINE! We've been in the same class since first grade and he lives to make my life a MISERY! (I think he's just jealous of my drawing skills.)

Mike is always surrounded by his goons:

Goon 1

CASSIE:
Laughs like a
hyena in pain.

Goon 2

PETE:
Big and not
too bright.

Goon 3

TYLER:
Eats nothing but
string cheese.

ME AND MEAN MIKE: <u>A BRIEF HISTORY</u>

Chapter 2 **The World's Worst Field Trip**

Soon ... "Okay everyone, on the bus!" said Mr. Squibb.

I couldn't wait to get to Fallout Island and do some sketching.

Maybe I'd get some cool ideas for my Space Ape comic!

Heh!

Trip!

Oof!

Drop!

"Now, Mike, you've already got three detentions this week

and it's only 10a.m. on Monday!" said Mr. Squibb.

You have your whole life to be a jerk! Why don't you just take a day off and give us a break?

Wow, that's the first time that anyone has ever talked to Mike that way!

On the bus...

So, I hear that Fallout Island is full of mutants!

You should fit in just fine, then! Haw haw!

THE ZOO CALLED! They want you back by 6p.m.!

FATAL BLOW!

+10 COMEBACK POINTS!!

Wow! She's so cool! And terrifying!

Did you know that starfish spew out their guts to digest their enemies outside of their bodies so they can fit them through their tiny mouths?

That's gross...

...but kind of cool!

I wasn't sure this was such a good idea. Blootonium? Giant bees? Carrot-onion hybrids?!

I was trying my best to ignore Mean Mike and his goons and do some sketching.

Okay class, we'll be at the island in ten minutes!

It'll be your EDUCATIONAL DOOM!!

Does his eyepatch keep switching eyes?

!!!

CHOMP!

CHOMP!

Three heads?!

Hee hee!

GLARE!

(again)

Let's go, kids!

And we were on <u>FALLOUT ISLAND!</u>

"Watch your step, children! Yar!"
said Captain Poopdeck.

"Captain, why does your
EYEPATCH keep
switching eyes?" I asked.

"I have no idea what ye be talking
about! Yar!" said Captain Poopdeck.

Mr. Squibb rounded us all up and we headed off. For a radiation-filled HAZARD, it was actually pretty scenic!

"Okay class, time for a hike! Pay particular attention to
the MUTATED flora!"

Field Trip Report

NAME: Andy

DATE: October 20

DESTINATION: Fallout Island

DESCRIBE THE VISIT (IN YOUR OWN WORDS): We looked at weird stuff

PICTURE AND NOTES:

QUESTIONS FOR CLASS DISCUSSION:

Shouldn't the Blootonium barrels be sealed??

Were those things on the cabbages EYES??

Oh, a squirrel!

CHITTER!

Hi there, little guy! Can I sketch you?

Waggle!

CHITTER CHITTER!

Ha ha! You're so cute!

SNATCH!

Nyeh!*

*Translation: Chump!

What the?! Who gets their pencil stolen by a squirrel? This can only end badly... I need to see what happens!

COME BACK HERE!!

!!!

Oh my! That doesn't look good!

Okay kids, back to the boat! Quick!!

Looks like dweeb and scary girl are going to miss the boat!

CAPTAIN POOPDECK!!

Well, they lasted longer than I thought they would!

And...

All aboard! Is that everyone?

24 ... 25! Yes, can we go now??

Good job Mr. Squibb is awful at math!

Heh!

Giant squirrel? Pah! I once saw a half-shark, half-crab, half-gator hybrid!

Yes, that math checks out just fine!

Meanwhile...

Maybe he's friendly?

STOMP!

By all means, stop and ask him!!

GIBBLE! GIBBLE!

If Squirrelzilla hadn't been chasing us, I would have stopped to SKETCH him! We ran through the woods back to the dock.

"Quick, through here! Maybe we can lose him!" I shouted.

Luckily, it looked like squirrelzillas weren't too INTELLIGENT!

I ran to grab my pencil.

"Wow, look at this!" I said.

"Never mind that thing! Run before that radiated rodent WAKES UP!!" shouted Mona.

Chapter 3 Escape from Fallout Island

But when we reached the dock...

Noooo!

"*NOOOO!*" I shrieked.

"They left without us! I don't believe this! Trapped on a radioactive island with a mutant squirrel! *GASP!* Maybe we'll mutate too!"

Mona sighed. "Oh, *CALM DOWN!* We just need to think logically about this. Here's your stupid giant pencil!"

"I don't want to live here and eat those weird carrot-onions forever!" I said.

"Stop being so DRAMATIC! It's a shame you can't draw yourself out of this!"

"Hmm, maybe I *CAN!*"

The boat I had drawn C A M E   T O   L I F E !

Mona poked it. "It's real!" she said. "Wow, I take back all of my sarcasm! The blootonium must have done something to your pencil!"

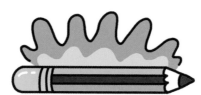

Just then, the monster reappeared.

"Oh no, Squirrelzilla woke up and now he looks even **ANGRIER!** We have to go!" I said.

"I think he wants your pencil," said Mona.

So long, fur face!

Phew!

Rabble gibble blabble!

CAW!

SPLAT!

Wow, I can't believe what just happened! It's like something out of issue 578 of *Unfeasible Gamma Guys!*

Wait, you like the Gamma Guys? I didn't think anyone else liked it!

Um, I mean...

Issue 578 features the Squirrel King! That's a very specific reference! Wait a second...

Umph!

"You're a SECRET DWEEB!"

"Okay, fine!"
said
Mona.
"Yeah,
I'm a dweeb!
What's wrong with that?"

"Nothing at all! EVERYONE should be a dweeb!" I replied.

Mona quickly changed the subject. "We should talk about this pencil and this boat. Will it get us back to the mainland?"

"I guess we'll find out," I said.

28

Oh! I guess we won't have to!

Hmm...

POP!

What?! How did they get back here?

Okay, back on the bus! If you could not mention the dangerous squirrel to your parents... heh...

whispers Also the giant magic pencil!

Hee hee!

On the bus...

I think we need to find out what this pencil can do! Here's my Splat-Chat username! When you get home, message me and we'll make a detailed investigation of its capabilities!

Can I send you my Gamma Guys fanfiction, too?

Sure, why not?

YAY!

During dinner, all I could think about was testing out my new pencil!

I wolfed down everything and headed to my room. "Finished! I'm off to do my HOMEWORK!"

"Dishes first," said Mom. Argh! "But my homework!" I whined.

MOM'S DEATH GLARE!

"OKAY, OKAY! DISHES!"

FINALLY, after the dishes were done, I raced to my room! "Come on, Taters!"

Tater-tot: BEST dog!

Stuff I drew with the pencil that came to life!

A sausage with legs

A friendly robot

Squishy octopus

A T. rex
(I made sure he was very small!)

A hand
(TERRIFYING!!)

SPLAT-CHAT V 2.0

ARTY GUY

So I drew a bunch of things with the pencil in my sketchbook and they all came to life!!

The radiation must have altered the molecular structure of the atoms in the pencil!

COOL GRRL

ARTY GUY

Uh... yeah... just what I was thinking! 😄

😊 Sure it was! How long did each doodle last before it disappeared?

COOL GRRL

ARTY GUY

Around 10 mins, which is good because I drew a hand and it was the scariest thing ever!!

Ha ha! Better watch what you draw! Hmm, maybe the bigger the sketch, the longer it lasts?

COOL GRRL

ARTY GUY

Makes sense! I have to go. See you @ school tomorrow!

Bring the pencil!! Also, your Gamma Guys fic was pretty cool!

COOL GRRL

Chapter 4   **Pencil Power!**

Of course, living with a little brother is a risk to magic pencil security ...

"What have you got?" Oscar asked.

"NOTHING! It's a ... project for school!" I said hastily.

I knew I'd get some funny looks at the bus stop but I didn't care—I had a magic pencil!

I messaged Mona when I got on the bus...

See you at school! I've got the pencil!

Awesome! I'll wait by the main gate!

Hey, I don't know how you and Scary Girl got back to the bus but I know that something fishy is going on!

BOINK!

I'm onto you, Dweeb!

SINK!

At school...

Hi!

Is that a golf bag?

You won't believe what this pencil can do!

Andy...

Look, we need to be really careful not to flash that thing around! Mean Mike already has his eye on you and if this pencil falls into the wrong hands...

I promise I'll be careful!

I'm serious! We need to be responsible.

Oh, come on...!

We can be responsible AND have a little fun? Responsible fun?

Hmm...

Fine...

Let's see what this pencil can do!

Yessss!

As soon as we got into class ...

"Ugh, I'm not ready for a POP QUIZ!" I groaned.

"Well, we do have a solution to that," Mona said with a grin.

"Set off the fire alarm?" I asked.

Mona rolled her eyes. "The PENCIL!"

⭐ FUN WE HAD WITH THE ⭐ PENCIL!

Drawing a gang of raccoons to chase Mean Mike and his goons!

ENTERTAINING THE SCHOOL WITH A GIANT DANCING PINEAPPLE!

FIREWORK DISPLAY!

THIS PENCIL IS...

⭐ ⭐

...100% AWESOME

Mr. Squibb and the principle were going crazy by the end of the day ...

"And then an

ELEPHANT

chased me

through the

cafeteria!"

"I didn't like that

DANCING PINEAPPLE one bit!"

Everyone was talking about it! I felt like I had the best secret in the world. Mona wasn't as enthusiastic about it though ...

"Okay, today has been fun and all but we really can't do anything like this again," she said.

"Oh, you worry too much! What

could **POSSIBLY**

go wrong with

a **MAGIC**
PENCIL

that makes art

come to life?"

ANDY!

Okay, I promise I'll be careful!

Come on, I've got a great idea for a Space Ape story!

Grumble!

I just know that those two are up to something! But what?

TAP

AAAHHH! A RACCOON!

Woah, it's just me!!

Back home ...

SCRIBBLE!

POP!

"This is so much fun! I love this pencil!"

Things were looking

so **SWEET** right now! Anything was

possible with this pencil. Maybe I could run for student president!

Andy!
Dinner!

President
ANDY!

Coming!

Uh-oh!

POP!

A MAGIC
PENCIL!

I woke up feeling great! I couldn't wait to do some more doodling!

BUT WAIT.

Um, WHERE'S MY PENCIL?

I'm sure the pencil was right here!

GONE!

Okay, don't panic! It must just be under my bed or in my closet...

But the pencil was GONE!

"Mona's going to be so totally unimpressed with me! I'll be hearing "I TOLD YOU SO" until the end of time!"

CRASH!

What was that?!

It came from Oscar's room!

Nice jammies!

"ANDY, BREAKFAST!" Mom called.

I quickly got dressed and grabbed the pencil. Running down the stairs, I pointed at Oscar.

"YOU!" I hissed.

You stole the pencil and made a monster!

Pfft, so what?

Mom came out of the kitchen.

"Everything okay, boys?" she asked.

"Heh heh, yeah! I'm just going to take Oscar to the park because I'm such a GOOD BROTHER!"

Hmm, okay. But take a piece of toast!

We raced out of the house and I told Oscar how much

TROUBLE he had caused.

"This is terrible! I'm the one who's going to be grounded until I'm an old man! Never mind the hole in the side of our house!"

We **RAN** down the street and as we rounded a corner we ran into...

Mean Mike and his gang! Ugh, this was all I needed!

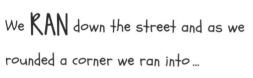

> Hey, it's Dweeb Face! What are you up to, Dork?

I really don't have time for this!

Hee hee!

Aw, he's babysitting!

> I still think you're up to something sneaky and I'll find out what it is!

I need to distract them quick but keep the pencil a secret!

Think fast!

Hey look! It's that guy from that band that you like!

Huh?

Okay, now's my chance while they're distracted...!

PENCIL GO!

There's nobody there!

Also, that was strangely non-specific!

POP!

What the— that looks like a real robot!

That's because it IS a real robot!

TRASH DETECTED!

Oof!!

Okay, that'll keep them busy and give the robot a chance to disappear!

Wow!

But ...

It's eaten the whole pencil factory and is heading for town! People are definitely going to notice!

I need to call Mona!

Beep boop beep!

Mona, it's—

A giant monster? Really, Andy?!

My little brother got hold of the pencil and made it!

Chew!

Okay okay! Just get over here now! I'm formulating a plan!

Okay...

Come on, pest!

I want the pencil again!

YANK!

At Mona's house ...

Come in!

I told Mom we need the basement for a role-playing game.

An RPG?

Hmpf.

I'm really sorry Mona!

You're really lucky that I work well under pressure!

Workstation!

MOUNTAINS

TOWN

Town Map!

GAMMA GUYS

PLAN

Wow!!

Diorama!

"This is **AMAZING!** How did you have time to do all of this?"

"It's not that different from planning a campaign for 'Crypts & Critters.' But never mind that..."

"It's like a proper operations room! You are the *COOLEST DWEEB* ever!"

Andy, focus! That scribble monster is trashing the town.

Worse than that, if it reaches the mountain range at the edge of town ...

REALLY REALLY BAD!!

Those mountains are made of pure graphite which is like one giant pencil! That thing will be unstoppable!

Oh.

This is all my fault! I feel TERRIBLE!

Sigh. Look, what's done is done but together we can fix this!

But how?

You have a magic pencil and an awesome imagination! We can draw a way to stop this thing!

I don't deserve a magic pencil. You should take it, Mona.

Andy, I may be smart, but I'm useless at drawing! You're a good artist—a SUPER artist. We'll work together to fix this!

You really think I'm a good artist?

I think you're cool, Andy!

Just don't let that go to your head!

I'm cool!

"**NOW,**" said Mona, all business again, "I took the liberty of designing you a costume.

Nobody can know you have a magic pencil.

Or, you know, realize that we're the cause of all this trouble."

"Gasp! Like a <u>REAL SUPERHERO!</u>"

"Here, SUPER DWEEB!

Go and get changed!"

said Mona.

"Super Dweeb?" I grumbled.

"Can't I have a cooler name?"

"Nope. I made the COSTUME, so I get to choose the name!"

"Hmph. Fair enough!"

"Okay, no more heroic posing" said Mona. "We need to stop that monster!"

"But... how? It's <u>HUGE!</u>" I said.

Mona handed me an earpiece. "Here, put this in your ear. I'll be right here to guide you and try to figure out how we can defeat that thing!"

We can do this!

YEAH!

Chapter 6 The Awesome Battle

Now, let's go get that monster!

Scribble!

POP!

All set!

Cool head set!

Onward, Birdy!

Good luck, Super Dweeb!

Soon...

Okay, we need a flat surface to draw on—let's land on one of those rooftops!

FLAP!

FLAP!

Thanks Birdy!

POP!

Time to draw this monster some "friends!"

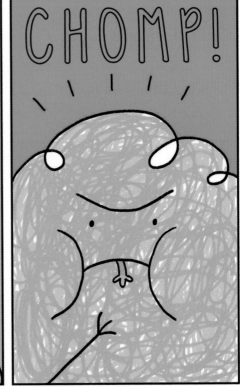

Mona, it isn't working! It's too strong!!

Just keep trying to distract it— I'm trying to figure something out!

Tap tap tap!

What have you done to the basement, Mona?!

It's for our RPG, Mom!

Well, I need to do the laundry!

What's this big hole?

Gasp! Yes! Sandymouth Canyon on the edge of town! Oscar, you're a genius!

If we can scare the monster into the canyon, it won't be able to eat any more graphite and after a while it'll disappear!

Okay, now we just need to work out what the monster is scared of!

BLORK!

What's the scariest thing I can draw? A zombie? A T. rex? A giant vampire? A tarantula?

The way you draw hands is pretty terrifying!

Come on, Mona! I need you to take this seriously!

I am taking it seriously! Draw the freaky hand!

POP!

Fine! BEHOLD! A badly drawn hand!

GROWL!

?!?!?!

BLAAARG!

Yes! It worked!

Good! Now chase it over to the canyon!

59

"Okay," said Mona, "now let's have a chat about

[RESPONSIBILITY!] "

"Heh heh!" I laughed. "Believe me, I think we've both

learned our lesson!"

RESPONSIBILITY!

"Fine," sighed Mona. "Well, HOPEFULLY we won't

have any more pencil-based excitement for a while.

And if anyone asks where we've been today, just give

them a MYSTERIOUS LOOK.

Oscar came to see me in my room.

Andy, I promise I won't take the pencil again!

"You know, I **MIGHT** need some help from time to time, not just with the pencil. You saved the day with your canyon idea," I said.

I really did, didn't I?

"Just don't let it go to your head, okay?"

WITH GREAT PENCIL COMES GREAT RESPONSIBILITY!

I think I've learned my lesson with the pencil. If my little brother could cause so much havoc with it, it can **NEVER** fall into the wrong hands!

Andy, dinner!

YUM!

Coming, Mom!

ROFF?

♪ DRAMATIC MUSIC! ♪

Fin!